T0194067

Nana Shirleyruth's Lovely Stories for Children, Teens, and Families

VOLUME 1

SHIRLEY DUKE SANMARTIN

Illustrated by Sierra Mon Ann Vidal

An endearing book of stories to read to your children to find courage when life gets scary, difficult or unfair; plus a great teenagers' story of temptation and living a life for God.

WESTBOW
PRESS®
A DIVISION OF THOMAS NELSON
& ZONDERVAN

Copyright © 2018 Shirley Duke SanMartin.

All rights reserved. No part of this book may be used or reproduced by any means, graphic, electronic, or mechanical, including photocopying, recording, taping or by any information storage retrieval system without the written permission of the author except in the case of brief quotations embodied in critical articles and reviews.

WestBow Press books may be ordered through booksellers or by contacting:

WestBow Press
A Division of Thomas Nelson & Zondervan
1663 Liberty Drive
Bloomington, IN 47403
www.westbowpress.com
1 (866) 928-1240

Because of the dynamic nature of the Internet, any web addresses or links contained in this book may have changed since publication and may no longer be valid. The views expressed in this work are solely those of the author and do not necessarily reflect the views of the publisher, and the publisher hereby disclaims any responsibility for them.

Any people depicted in stock imagery provided by Getty Images are models, and such images are being used for illustrative purposes only.
Certain stock imagery © Getty Images.

ISBN: 978-1-9736-4163-6 (sc)
ISBN: 978-1-9736-4162-9 (e)

Print information available on the last page.

WestBow Press rev. date: 11/12/2018

Contents

We are Soft, We are Loved, Touch Toes

It was evening and the stars outside brought soft light into this the children's room.

Three little stuffed animals talked while cuddled together in the little red rocking chair by the open window. Teddy, (who was really a big old long haired, button-eyed teddy bear), Pannie Bear,(who was really a fat but very tough Panda bear) and Bunny, (a small orange rabbit with lovely orange eyes and a head that flopped around, were best buddies They all stretched out towards each other saying their most favorite words in the whole world. "We are soft, we are loved, touch toes."

They were cottony soft and huggable; everybody loved them. When their toes touched it tickled but made them feel very brave. Close by, Eddie, Tommy and Betty, the little people, slept in their own comfy beds. Most of the toys were asleep also. Here in the children's room all was quiet; all was peaceful.

What a day of adventure it had been. The three children and their favorite little stuffed animals had spent the day rushing around a fairy castle, getting rid of bad dragons that tried to steal the fairies away.

It all happened in the back yard under an enormous apple tree. Betty sat on a wide royal swing with her dress flowing out to the grass below. "We need peace in this land", she had shouted. "All bad dragons, go away, go away".

The fairy castle was surrounded by three stout evergreens. Eddie and Tommy ran around with their brave Teddy and Pannie Bear trying to scare the dragons away with wild words and big sticks. They even rolled around getting pretty dusty and covered with grass stains. At last, the dragons said, "We're going away. You jump too high, you shout too loud and you punch too hard. You can have your peace and all those silly fairies, too." They left and it was so good.

Betty had hidden the fairies with Bunny under her enormous ball gown. Eddy and Tommy were glad they scared the naughty beasts away. In celebration, a royal banquet was given. Ivy crowns were given to the children and blue bows to their brave helpers.

"You may come back any time you wish and enjoy more milk and cookies with us," said the fairy queen. "Maybe we can help you some day."

All joined in for the triumphant march home.

They told the other toys all that had happened. Teddy helped Eddy by pretending to be a loud screaming monster. Pannie Bear helped Tommy push the dragons away with one fist then one leg then all of him. Those dragons sure did run away. Bunny was sweet and comforting. He kept blinking his sparkly eyes convincing the scared fairies to hide under Betty's gown. He kept flopping his head from one side to the other as he promised them, "It will be all over soon."

The other toys admired the blue bows and wished they could have helped, too.

Each had been part of some other amazing adventures: the horse on wheels had been to the wild west; the tiger and the elephant to the jungle; the many cars to races and trips to the city and the farm; the dolls to school, tea parties, plays.

They loved the children and tried to look their best so as to be chosen for the next make-believe story. Everything became so real. As they started to go to sleep, all they could hear was the buddies,

"We are soft, we are loved, touch toes."

Outside the room, footsteps could be heard. The door opened slowly, slowly and in the dark a tall something came in and looked at the children, then at the little red rocking chair at the little ones touching toes. Long arms stretched out and grabbed Teddy, Pannie Bear and Bunny. All the toys in the room were terrified. They thought the dragons had sent this tall something. It left with Teddy, Pannie Bear and Bunny.

The door closed.

Toys have voices when they need them. They called out for help, but the children were sleeping soundly and heard nothing.

However, the fairies heard and came. They were so sorry. They were sure all was because of them. Now it must be that the dragons were mad at the children and at the three little friends who had just been kidnapped. Far away they heard sounds like water and big voices. Maybe the thief was going to find a boat and take the little creatures off to the land of the dragons.

Some of the fairies stayed to comfort the toys while others went through the door and flitted out toward the sounds, down the stairs, through the kitchen to the back washroom. They saw two people laughing with scrub brushes, lots of soapy suds and Teddy, Panni Bear and Bunny all looking very surprised.

"I wouldn't dare trying to take these little ones away during the day, but we must get them all clean and get them back quickly. These blue ribbons will look better, too." It was the children's parents. They rolled the little soft animals in a big yellow towel, put them on a table, and used a fan to dry them off. The fairies saw how dazed their little friends were. As soon as the parents left the washroom, the fairies whispered words of comfort telling how the toys in the bedroom called out for their help.

"We were scared at first," said Teddy.

"I was ready to fight, but then I saw the nice people who love the children," said Pannie Bear.

"I now remember little people do this water and suds things, so it's OK for us, too," added Bunny. "Thank you for trying to come and help us. Please tell the others."

With all the strength the fairies had, they pushed the three little friends close to each other so they could touch toes and feel brave. Then they flew back to the children's room, and told what had happened.

As they lifted their wings to leave, they reminded the toys, "Call us anytime you need us. Good-bye." After they left, the toys in the children's room listened quietly and could hear happy sounds from far away.

"We are soft, we are loved, touch toes."

The buddies would be fine, back and ready for the next day.

Ally's Song

While still in her cocoon, a butterfly named Ally received a beautiful angelic message.

As she was starting to struggle out of her cozy home, she heard heavenly music and a loving gentle voice, " Little Ally, you have been chosen to bring joy to a very sick little girl. Her name is Becky. You are to bring her beauty and delight as her time on earth is short."

In her tiny heart, Ally already knew her very own time on earth would be very short also.

Here she could make her little one-day-life count. "I want to help, dear angel. Help me find Becky."

As Ally spoke with the angel, she saw a vision of the bright magnificent heaven with many angels hovering near. They were singing songs of love and adoration. "I love this and I want to sing these same beautiful songs, soft and high and magnificent."

The angel reassured Ally butterflies really do have voices. This new little yellow creature found her own song. It was sweet with a touch of heaven. Her sounds were so soft only butterflies and very small creatures could have ever heard it.

Now the moment of destiny was arriving. Ally struggled, twisting her little self and turning with all her might. She was on a mission. With one last great effort she burst up and out of her cocoon. She fluttered her sparkling yellow wings and rose up into the air, surrounded by brilliance, floating in the sunlight.

The wind caught her. A soft breeze, blown by the angel, carried her to a nearby garden filled with flowers and a shade tree. This must be the place. She fluttered her wings, then coasted down down to some daisies. The pretty white and yellow flowers were growing right beside a pale little girl seated on a soft red cushion. The seven year old had long dark hair and large blue eyes . She smiled as she listened to a lady beside her in a wicker chair reading to her. "This is what I like to do, reading your favorite Bible stories and talking about them." The lady looked up from her book and said softly, "I love you, Becky".

The little girl blew a kiss, then spoke weakly saying, "I love you, too, Mommy; please keep telling me about how much God loves me."

Then Becky saw Ally and her eyes sparkled. She smiled with complete delight as the little yellow butterfly twirled in the air, then danced with the daisies as gentle breezes came by. Ally sang the heavenly song she had just learned. She went to the little girl and rested on her arm, swaying back and forth, back and forth.

"Look, Mommy, This little butterfly wants to be my friend."

Becky's mother had often seen other butterflies coming to the garden, but they always flew away quickly. Ally stayed.

Ally's tiny heart was filled with joy and she wanted Becky to have some of that same delight. It was her mission, her life's purpose; she sighed, "I wish you could hear me and sing with me, Becky!"

The little girl had been praying for happiness. She wasn't strong at all. She wished she could run around and play and help her mother. It was getting hard to breathe some days. She used to love to sing. Times in the garden were precious to her. She used to plant and care for blue bachelor buttons, red and yellow moss roses and the daisies beside her. She loved the aroma from her mother's rose garden by the wall. The little fountain in the corner welcomed thirsty little birds.

She did not know this would be her last hour on earth.

For a long time, her mother watched as Becky and Ally delighted in each other. Becky would hum and Ally tried to flutter around to match the rhythms. Ally flew from Becky's arm to her outstretched hand, alighting on first one then another finger.

In the late afternoon, softly and beautifully Becky felt surrounded by a brilliant light. She looked at Ally and could even hear her heavenly song. It was wonderful. She could hear the heavenly choirs and see the angels welcoming her ready to bring her to God. She even saw hundreds, no, thousands of butterflies, all colors, dancing in the air and singing.

Becky smiled at her mother and whispered, "Heaven is so beautiful. I can see it. I'll sing for you again. I love you. " The little girl's spirit left.

Ally lifted her wings and went with her.

Ally, the butterfly, had given her whole life of one day. She was chosen to do this.

Years later when Becky's mother lost all her strength, she also heard the music and saw heaven, the butterflies and the angels. She ran in her spirit to her daughter. Becky was laughing and waiting with a beautiful little yellow butterfly on her shoulder.

All joined in to sing heavenly songs.

Millie and Bess

It was Wednesday afternoon. Earlier that day a kind lady bought a surprise from the Joy Store and had the secret protected in a wide yard of brown wrapping paper. She chuckled to herself as she carried it home.

A new little doll with blue eyes that opened and closed tried to look very sweet as she was unwrapped and placed on a golden velvet fringed pillow. There was laughter and squeals of delight from seven year old Bess when she saw her birthday present, a new doll. The girl's little tears of happiness fell on the doll's face. Bess covered her with kisses all over her face and hands and toes. This amazing gift doll enjoyed the wet surprise. Quickly she learned she enjoyed being picked up and held; also, Bess's soft squeezes seemed to be like real love and promises of more love.

It felt so good to be loved that much.

Bess brought her into the playroom where she received her own beautiful name, Millie, and was then properly introduced to the toys and dolls who lived there.

She was even introduced to the big tabby cat, Rufus, who walked all around and purred a nice welcome.

Millie looked around the play room. The other toys and dolls welcomed her and let out a happy sigh when she came. People could not hear it, but Millie could, and she felt this was where she belonged forever.

Nobody was perfect and Bess told all her toys and dolls that no matter what, she saw them as perfect. So as they got a little worn or torn a bit, they were still all princes and princesses to her. That made them feel good. Rufus knew he was perfect anyway.

After a few weeks, one of Millie's eyes was a little slow to open and close and the little doll started to worry about getting old. Bess loved her so much, she told her doll that she had just learned the precious art of winking and not to worry.

Everyone in the playroom sighed their approval. The kind lady who had bought Millie was Bess's mother and she wanted to do something new and special for her little girl. Secretly she measured, cut and sewed. When she was finished, she was thinking how she wished someone had done this for her when she was little.

That evening when it was story time, Bess's mother retold the story of Red Riding Hood. This was one of the child's favorite stories. When she finished, she asked Bess to bring Millie over to her. Then she proceeded to give her daughter a perfect little red velvet riding hood for Millie. It fit beautifully and had a crystal button on the front. Millie would have cried for happiness but she wasn't made with tears, so she just winked and winked for joy.

Bess was so happy about her own little Millie Red Riding Hood, she decided she would show it to her teacher and schoolmates that very next day. Rufus watched as she left to go walking to the school around the corner.

As she approached the schoolyard in front of the big main door, one of her classmates, Alice, saw the doll and in a jealous moment grabbed Millie. Then she hurried in to the school to tell the teacher and the other classmates that her mother had made the Red Riding Hood for this her doll. Bess was horrified. Millie was horrified. Bess sobbed explaining it was really her own doll and no one believed her. She cried. How could life be so unfair? Millie was scared to be taken away from so much love and protection.

Bess hugged Rufus when she got home and appreciated his warmth and loud purrs. She told the toys and dolls what had happened, and tried to comfort them with hugs for all. They all sighed, but this time with sadness.

The next morning Bess's mother went to the school. The little girl, Alice, that claimed Millie as her own, had just transferred to another school at another part of the city. The teacher did not know the exact address, but she thought she knew the general area. Bess's mother thanked her for the information as she made a mental note to do a little follow-up.

Bess's mother liked to visit some of the shut-in's at her church. A few days after the problem at the school, she took a bus to visit a sweet lady she had known for years, now confined to a wheelchair. She brought some chocolates and a little bouquet of violets and had a delightful visit with her old friend. As she was leaving, she wondered about the little girl, Alice's, new address. She realized she was in the same area mentioned by Bess's teacher. Was this a coincidence?

She noticed a garage sale going on down the street a way. She walked down just to check out the bargains. A lady was there with a table full of items that were surplus to her. Bess's mother looked and saw something winking at her from under old toys and clothes. Gently, she reached and pulled out Millie and asked how much for this used doll. The lady said, "I don't know where this came from, but my daughter has plenty of dolls, so I'm getting rid of it and some old toys. A dollar and it's yours."

Without any discussion, Bess's mother found a dollar, bought the doll and put Millie in her big purse. She kept giving her little squeezes all the way home. She brushed off any dust that had accumulated, she combed her hair, and brought her into the play room. Rufus jumped up to give her a lick as she was placed with all the other toys and dolls. Oh the beautiful sighs. The beautiful Millie Red Riding Hood was home.

When Bess came home from school, she was still very sad. She missed her darling Millie. She went to try to cheer up the other toys and dolls in the playroom.

There were sparkles greeting her, one from a crystal button and others from two blue eyes, one of which was happily winking and winking in excitement. Rufus let out an amazing "meow" as Bess ran to hug her beautiful Millie Red Riding Hood.

Home is a wonderful place.

Boston 1911

CHAPTER 1

The Beginning

It was Boston in February 1911. There was a sprinkling of snow on the ground, not melting, just there. The day was freezing, clear with occasional breezes chilling all who ventured out. This was the long-awaited Saturday of the Methodist Youth rally. There was laughter and excitement in the air. Young people from Boston and the surrounding communities were planning to gather together to enjoy this experience. For many it was the highlight of the year.

All looked forward to joyful singing, Bible teaching, speakers, reports from missions trips, then lunch, games and contests led by the youth pastors. This was to be an all-day event for teenagers and for young men and women in their twenties.

Anita and her friends, Jennie and Ethel, took the trolley early that morning from Mattapan to the big Union United Methodist church near the Boston Public Gardens. The girls were only 15, but they had traveled this way many times before with their parents.

Anita kept saying, "I could hardly sleep last night."

Jennie added, "I kept the kerosene lamp going on low all night I was so afraid I'd be late and I just can't miss all the fun. I love thinking about going all the way to Boston, just the three of us."

"I've had my outfit ready for days", Ethel added. "I want to look nice and feel grown up." She smoothed her new bright blue scarf draped casually around her neck. Her matching gloves reflected her deep blue eyes; her long black wool coat was like a moving silhouette. "Mom and Dad trust me as long as I stay close to both of you. They wonder if I could do something silly if I had a little too much freedom. They know all about my imagination." She giggled and winked. "But, I'll be good."

The girls were beautiful. They all had long wavy hair. Anita was dressed in rose and Jennie in white. They appreciated their wool coats that kept them toasty warm. They moved gracefully and locked arms after they stepped off the trolley. They loved being together. They had to keep each other from falling avoiding small patches of slick ice along the sidewalk.

Anita cried out, "There it is!"

The church was spread out over half of a block. The spires were majestic. The church bells rang. The girls held hands as they climbed the well worn stone steps. The doors were heavy and wide, yet welcoming all who entered. The lights were soft and the stained glass windows gave a holy atmosphere to the sanctuary. This was where the main meetings were to be held.

"This makes me want to sing something loving to God. He is so good and cares for us all the time," whispered Jennie.

There was a side stairway leading to a lower floor. The girls went down to find a warm pleasant activities room. Many tables had been prepared, decorated with red and white gingham tablecloths and daisies in short blue vases. Ethel pointed out a kitchen off to one side with some older ladies bustling around making their salads and pies.

Anita walked over to an enormous coat closet next to the stairs. "Here we are, come on. I'm too warm to stay all bundled up."

The girls hung up their coats and stuffed their hats, scarves and gloves into the sleeves. They turned noticing how the room was set up for the lunch later on.

Ethel remarked, "It's going to be good, very good."

"I'm hungry already!" added Jennie.

"You, my adorable friends, are always hungry. Remember, all in good time," said Anita. "Let's go back upstairs and get seats near the front. We can see everything better that way."

Hearts racing they went back up the stairs to the sanctuary resplendent with beauty, pipe organ music, and soft red cushions on the pews. The girls sat near the front and clapped their hands in delight as they saw many had come and others were just arriving. Their own youth minister, Pastor Baker, was greeting all the different groups as they came through the main entrance. He directed them to the coat closets and encouraged them to settle in quickly and get ready for a great day of fellowship.

Hundreds of young men and women enjoyed the morning of music and messages. One youth group sang "When I survey the wondrous cross, on which the Prince of glory died, my richest gain I count but loss and pour contempt on all my pride..." It was inspiring to hear teenagers singing such a moving message. All the verses were clear with God's truth.

Another church sent a group of musicians to play some of the newer songs, and everyone joined in. Anita especially loved the piano expansive interpretation portions. She herself had been learning to play, and yearned to do better and better. She hoped to bless others with her music some day.

Pastor Ellis, The young minister from nearby Jamaica Plain, gave a message that touched many hearts. "God forgives and loves us completely. He always has and always will. He reaches out to us giving us enough faith to ask Him to save us from evil and the evil one." Perceptive souls could understand this young man was speaking from experience, from walking with and enjoying the presence of the Lord in his life.

He continued, "Through that faith in Jesus Christ, God comes to your souls to live and guide your precious lives. He promises us a beautiful eternity in heaven with Him and all the other souls that choose Him."

Pastor Ellis went on encouraging the young people to repent, regret their failures, ask forgiveness from God, accept that complete forgiveness and open their hearts to God. He explained all about Jesus' sacrifice that made it even possible to be part of the family of God.

"Look forward to the adventure called 'life' ". He read Bible verses so all could hear the truth right from God's Word.

"God has a perfect plan for your life. Trust Him. Don't miss out on the best He has for you.

"There is a great hymn called 'Trust and Obey'. The words will help you. The chorus goes: 'Trust and Obey, for there's no other way, to be happy in Jesus, but to trust and obey.'" Everyone joined in a spontaneous singing of that chorus and then the pastor closed his eyes and prayed for all who had come.

One of the long expected features of the morning program came next. All listened to a presentation from some teenagers who had gone on a missions trip along with several parents. This particular group from four different churches, had traveled to the Appalachian area the summer before. They saw as their mission to help the very poor with church construction. At the same time, they brought many boxes of nutritious food. Several teens were talented musicians so they shared and taught music to their beloved new mountain friends. In turn, two of the Appalachian men played their home made instruments. The never- to- be-forgotten highlights were the evening Bible studies. Because it was all about God, it was good.

One of the young men, Larry, explained how lives were changed forever; not only for the mountain folks but also for every teen and team member who had given the summer over to serving others.

One of the parents who had helped supervise the trip showed large blown up pictures of some of the happenings; it was easy to notice everyone was happy. It was a life changing experience, not only for the poor who were helped, but also for those who were glad to serve others above themselves.

Larry explained they all tried to be the hands of Jesus, say the words of Jesus, do the acts of kindness of Jesus, just letting God shine through them. As the service ended many young people felt inspired to be not so selfish and do something wonderful with their lives.

It was obvious that this was something that could be done by most of those who were there. About twenty signed up for the next year's mission trip resolving to save up their funds to make the trip.

Part of the last song was "I'd rather have Jesus, than silver or gold." Anita, along with many others, sang with all her heart. God heard that. It was good.

Jennie pulled the girls along with her to go downstairs. "I am just so hungry."

A nice lunch was being served. The girls were in high spirits and appreciated the nice chicken casserole and salad. They sat together giggling and then started looking across the room. Some of the boys were all sitting together and seemed to be shy and not inclined to introduce themselves to others. One would think they were afraid of girls with their impulsive unnerving surprising puzzling manners. They were going to protect themselves from female mushy mind games.

Ethel hatched up a plan and took out some slips of paper. The girls each wrote out their own names and phone numbers and slyly moved over to the coat closet. They quickly found three coats that must have belonged to boys and each stuck a paper in a pocket. They walked out of the closet nonchalantly, then sat down to eat the apple pie that was just being served.

During and after dessert time, Anita, Jennie and Ethel had lots of fun playing silly games with many others. They forgot about being shy and made some new friends.

All returned upstairs for a final sing-along and encouraging message from Pastor Baker. He spoke about how God had plans for each life and He would bring things together for His purposes, in His time. Each person should pray for God's perfect will.

The girls felt sad the day was ending and said their good-byes to the new and old friends they met during the day. They hurried to get their coats. When they got to the closet, they noticed the boys' coats were gone. They wondered what those boys were like. Where did they go? What was going to happen now? Proper young ladies doing something so wrong and unusual as sharing their names and phone numbers was their special secret. They agreed to never tell anyone and pretend it never happened.

It was going to get dark before long. They hustled and caught the next trolley and returned home.

Ethel trudged up the steps of her home. As she opened the front door she was glad to find her mother waiting for her. That welcoming hug made her feel comfortable and safe. It was a special blessing to have a loving praying parent. (In fact, both of her parents loved the Lord).

Ethel shared news of the day and how much the messages touched her heart. Her father came to the dining table to hear it all over again. It made him remember some of the church meetings that changed his life from selfishness to compassion. He was glad that was while he was a young man he dedicated himself to following

Jesus. He smiled to himself, glanced over at his wife knowing she was part of God's plan for his life. After a brief prayer of thanks, a nice bowl of hot soup and toast, they were ready to call it a day.

Ethel was ready to just throw herself down on the bed. She was tired but the name "Larry" kept coming to her imaginative mind. Oh, yes, Larry was that dreamy fellow who spoke at the convention about the Appalachian missions trip. She wondered if he could ever be part of God's plan for her life. "Larry, Larry, what a nice guy" she murmured softly, "Larry, Larry, are you the one....?"Then she remembered her idea of putting the slips of paper in boys' coats. She realized her imagination exaggerated all her romantic ideas. "What was I thinking? I hope God isn't mad at me."

She was excited just thinking and remembering her day in Boston. Eventually, she nodded off to sleep.

Now, in turn, Jennie also was glad to be back home as it was getting extremely cold. She kept humming some of the songs she heard that day. As she hung up her coat and put away her gloves and scarf, she kept thinking about the messages that really touched her heart. She found her parents in the living room.

"Mom and Dad, thanks for letting me go to Boston with Anita and Ethel. We had such a good time; lots of young people were there. I loved all the music. I just kept singing and singing all the hymns and songs. I knew all of them. I think maybe I'll try out for the choir so I can learn more."

"You have a lovely clear voice, my dear. Maybe this is how God wants you to bless others."

"Thanks, Mom, I'll pray about this tonight. Pastor Baker spoke about how God had plans for each life and He would brings things together for His purposes, in His time. Each person should pray for God's perfect will."

"I really want God's perfect plan for my life, maybe music, maybe my own family, maybe a job where what I do can make a real difference in this world. Most of all, I want to get closer to my Lord and Savior. We were encouraged to pray and read the Holy Bible. God gives comfort and wisdom and help in the hour of need."

Jennie's father shared how much he had been praying for his only daughter to discover the same holy secrets he had found as a young man. He remembered dedicating his life to God.

"Give thanks to God as he shows you a direction. You should choose a career you love and study hard. You will never be alone, honey, no matter what happens."

"You are so good to me, Dad. I've figured out you and Mom are part of God's perfect plan for my life. I'm glad of that. I guess I'll take it one day at a time, but right now, one night at a time." Jennie started yawning, "I am getting so sleepy after my long day in Boston. Good night and God bless you." The warm hugs ended the day and Jennie went to bed.

A little earlier in the evening, Anita had said "Good-bye" to her dear friends, Ethel and Jennie. She hurried down the street from the trolley stop to her home. Her parents, brothers and sisters were all inside waiting for her.

"Come on in, you must be freezing," exclaimed her mother.

"Yeah, Anita's home, Anita's home" welcomed her little sister, Ruthie and her brother, Charlie. They ran to hug her. Squeezing Anita always made them feel good.

The whole family was sharing hot cocoa with marshmallows and homemade raisin bread at the big round table in the dining room. The inviting aroma filled the home. Laughter and happy voices made home seem like a bit of heaven on earth. It was a blessing to see so many family members with abundant love for each other..

Anita hung up her rose colored coat in the hall closet and turned to all the happy faces. They were glad she had a great time with her friends all the way into Boston. She shared the messages from the young pastors and told about the helpful missions trip right here in the United States. She explained how everyone should help the poor and encourage those who are in need.

Since the next day was Sunday, all the children prepared their clothes for church in the morning. Anita did, too, and prayed for her heart to be prepared also for the next message from God. It was good getting into bed under her inviting patchwork quilt. Although she was very drowsy, she could not go right off to sleep.

CHAPTER 2

The Big Worry

Anita felt very worried that what she and her friends had done was wrong. It was pretty wild just putting her name and phone on a piece of paper to be stuffed in an unknown person's pocket. She was terrified she might get a call from a strange young man. As she drifted off to sleep she struggled. Whatever should she do? Whatever should she say?

It became an unnecessary problem for Jennie and Ethel. They asked God to please forgive them. They never heard from anyone, and in their repentant hearts they were glad.

But Anita did. When the telephone call came, somehow she managed to act like a normal human being. She was peaceful and kind. She mentioned how much she enjoyed the rally, and then even agreed to meet that mysterious young man. He told her he liked her voice, that it was sweet and musical. Her heart was pounding and she had tears in her enormous hazel eyes. He sounded sort of nice, but how in the world could she know. She was beyond scared.

When the day and time came to meet, she could not go through with it. She had a feeling she escaped something, maybe something very dangerous or not quite right.

She was only fifteen. That was the end of that.

CHAPTER 3

Growing Up

That cured her of her wild adventurous imaginations for years. She just kept on finishing her high school studies and improved her piano playing. It was a delight to practice every day. Anita had a sweet nature and loved being the accompanist at Sunday School and all her youth meetings at her church. She was grateful she was able to do that. Her musical ability was a gift from God and she loved sharing. Sometimes she would fill in for the organist as needed some Sunday mornings in the large sanctuary. It took a while learning to use more than one keyboard, and then the big foot pedals. It was another type of sound and she hoped it pleased the Lord in heaven.

Faithfully, every year she would go to the Methodist Youth Rally. No more notes in boys' coat pockets. She loved all the pastors' messages and got to know some of the piano players from other churches. She even went to a church mission project for the poor in Appalachia for three weeks one summer.

That year Ethel went with her. They found they could have lots of fun in doing hard work and making a difference. Anita watched

Ethel as she finally met Larry, now the leader of this particular mission endeavor. This was the same Larry her friend had dreamed about when she first saw him talking about the Appalachian project at the youth rally. They had lots in common: a sense of humor, a will to get things done, a love for the people they came to help. Anita was glad for them as she saw God's perfect plan emerging.

CHAPTER 4

Ten Years Later

One year, 1921, after the Great War was over, more and more young people planned to come to the yearly rally. This time one church sent their special music group to play in the morning meeting. The instruments they played were the violin, the cello and the piano.

Anita was there early as usual. She had encouraged many of the teens from her church to be there. They were settling in on their own.

Anita was there when a message came that the piano player was ill and the little group needed someone to fill in.

Anita stepped up. She found out that she knew the music they were going to play. She had played those songs many times at her church. The violin player was tall, probably in his late twenties, blue eyed, a kind yet intense look on his face.

"My name is Tom and this is Allen. He's been playing the cello for about five years. Sorry about our pianist. He hated to miss this meeting but when you're sick, you're sick and had better take it easy."

Anita was pleased to meet them. They went over the songs and went through a short practice run before the meeting even began. Anita knew how to improvise and not overpower the other musicians.

The rally began. The music was beautiful. Most of the people there did not know the three had never played together before.

At lunchtime, the musicians sat down together. Anita said, "I'm so glad to meet you both. Tell me about yourselves and your church."

Allen didn't say much, ate quickly and excused himself as he saw some old friends.

Tom seemed happy to have Anita to himself. He told how he had been coming to the youth rallies off and on for about 10 or 11 years. He loved being part of the music ministry at his church. He had been in the Army during the Great War, survived and now he was a teacher in one of the elementary schools in his town.

"I love teaching history and geography. I want the youngsters to know the truth about our founding fathers and how they committed their lives to God asking Him for wisdom.

"Also, God made a beautiful world and the more we study other lands, the more we can marvel at His creation. Personally, I long to reach the unbelieving souls scattered throughout so many countries. I'm not sure how right now. However, in the meantime I hope I can encourage my students to make a difference in their own lives. Their dedication to truth will bring them far, on to the best plan God can have for them and the lives they affect.

"War is terrible and I saw too much suffering, greed, misunderstanding and lots of evil. I thank God He guided me every day and spared me for a future of service to others."

Anita listened thoughtfully. This was a man of faith and she was glad to have met him.

"I prayed a lot for all the soldiers during the war, so that covers you, too, Tom. I'm glad you survived all that horror. You are a hero in my eyes."

Anita listened closely as this friendly young man shared many other thoughts. She loved listening to him.

"I've been playing the violin for many years and it is just another part of me wanting to share the beauty of music."

"I know the feeling, Tom. That is the way I feel about playing the piano. It seems to honor God, so I try to do my best every time. I'm glad we could do the music for the morning meeting."

Anita told how she worked in an office for the Quaker Oats Company. She helped support her mother, brothers and sisters after her father died just after her high school graduation. Her great loves were art and music. She had to forget about going to college to study to become an art teacher; but every week she was able to play piano at her church. She even gave lessons to a few children.

She went on. "My friend Jennie married a movie theatre owner. He asked me to play the piano sometimes for the silent movies."

Tom laughed as she told how she could make people scared or worried or excited or sad by the way she played. Jennie's husband often said, "Make 'em weep, Anita, make 'em weep."

Tom continued," I've always loved music and loved learning the violin. I play all I can at my church. I guess now I could play any emotion as you did for the silent movies. I could make the violin sound sad or happy, ominous or excited. But most of all, I love playing the old hymns."

Anita smiled.

The rally resumed and at the end of the day, Tom asked Anita for her name and phone number so he could call her some day. She scratched it off on a slip of paper. She watched as he put it into his wallet.

"Would he really call her?" She thought. "He seemed like a caring person and I feel pretty comfortable talking with him. He must be like that with everyone, though, so I'll just let it go and keep on keeping on."

He did call her and she was glad.

After about three months of phone calls and even some dates, Anita felt she had been blessed to have found a godly friend.

They liked going for walks around the Boston Commons, feeding the ever hungry pigeons with some saved bread scraps. There were lonely people on the many benches amongst the trees, so they tried to give a cheery word or two, leaving a little Bible tract with eternal messages and a couple of chocolate candies. They were like sunshine to many sad darkened souls.

After a few hours walking around, they loved stopping for coffee and English muffins. Sometimes they went to their special donut place that had a motto "Wherever you may wander, whatever be your goal, keep your eyes upon the donut and not upon the hole." Good philosophy; it kept them laughing.

Knowing Anita loved art, Tom brought her to the Boston Museum of Fine Arts several times. Then, on one occasion, they attended a mini concert by a string quartet at the Isabella Stewart Gardner Museum. Hearing such melodic pieces in the midst of many beautiful paintings brought music and art together. There was an inner courtyard there with many plants, trees and flowers enhancing the whole experience.

He came out to her home to meet her family. Before long, all joined in as the two happy musicians played songs and hymns. Anita's skill in playing the piano now changed from trying to do her best to letting out the music in her soul. Tom had an inner joy in praising God through the violin and finding the way to bring special new harmonies to each piece. It was a delightful experience. They liked playing together and did it well.

Anita's mother kept watching and praying for her beloved daughter. She wanted the plan God had chosen for each of her children. She hoped they could handle rejection and disappointment in their own dreams, knowing God has it all worked out in the end. It was like the hymn, Trust and Obey".

It seemed there was no end to what Tom and Anita could talk about. It seemed they had similar interests and a desire to learn more. Most of all, they loved to share what God was revealing in His holy word. They were learning to appreciate His kindnesses in their lives.

One afternoon in April, Tom called and said he had something to show her.

She could not imagine what he had in mind.

"Probably some new music we could play together." She thought.

She called Jennie and explained, "He is really such a good friend. I am glad that other piano player could not be part of the ensemble that day at the convention, (but, of course, I am sorry he was sick). It is just so comfortable going on long walks with Tom. We have so much in common and I do like his jokes. Playing music together takes us into another world that only musicians can understand. Sharing the love of Jesus makes him a good Christian brother. We share the new thoughts God gives us from the Holy Bible."

Jennie replied,"It is a gift from God to have real Christian brothers and sisters. You and Ethel have been there for me all the way. We went through so much as teenagers. I knew God had a plan for my life and look at wonderful Frank, my husband. It took me a while to see he was part of God's plan for me, but I can see clearly now. He is my sweet husband and best friend. I get horrified thinking of our wild ideas of meeting a stranger, (remember how we put our phone numbers in the boys' coat pockets)."

"I love talking with you, Jennie. Life is not easy for me trying to care for my mother and my younger sister and brother. My other sister and brothers are doing the best they can and have young families to care for. I enjoy friendships, but I must walk the lonely road. I will always serve the Lord in my heart and through music. I love my coworkers at my job and I try to do the best I can. I guess that is the plan for my life."

"Take care, Anita, and keep your heart open for God's surprises."

"You are so cute. See you later, Bye."

"Bye."

Anita took her time getting ready to see Tom again. She wore her soft dusty rose dress and a single strand of pearls her mother gave her. She pushed her wavy hair back and when she looked in the mirror, she saw a twinkle in her large hazel eyes.

Late that afternoon Anita met Tom at the Boston Music store. It always seemed to have a friendly atmosphere. The couple was excited going over the sheet music sold there. Sometimes in the past, they had each bought several items for music for their churches.

Tom said," I'm a bit hungry, how about you?"

"Why, yes, a bit, just like you."

"I have an idea; let's go down this side street."

They went to a little Italian restaurant and sat in a quiet corner. By now Tom knew Anita's favorite dish and ordered. They loved the Italian opera being played in the background.

After they finished spaghetti, meatballs and salad, they laughed.

"Not a drop of Italian blood in me, but I love this food, "said Tom.

"Me, too."

Slowly, Tom took out his wallet and said "Better late than never." Anita was puzzled and wondered what he meant. She loved his mysterious smile and his mysterious words.

Tom pulled out a couple of papers from his wallet and showed them to Anita. Both had her name and phone number and in her handwriting.

Unbelievable.

She blushed at the memory of the older one and was happy about the second one. Anita laughed nervously remembering the 1911 youth rally.

"I thought I was very brave to put that in your coat pocket. I apologize. After you called, I just couldn't meet you or anyone like that. I was just too young, too scared and in the end, I wanted to do the right thing. I've never done anything like that ever again. Remember the pastor talked about finding the plan for your life and I felt so guilty."

"Anita, I looked forward to that meeting. Your voice seemed so sweet it spoke to my soul. When you didn't come, I just thought maybe, some day I would find you. I kept your name and phone number anyway. I kept it in my wallet all the time. I kept thinking there must have been a reason for all of this. I even kept it with me while I was in France during the War. I just couldn't seem to throw it away."

"When you gave me your name and phone number last February, I thought my heart would stop. I listened closely and heard that same sweet musical voice coming back to me; it has been delightful getting to know you."

Tom reached across the table and took her hand. "I know I am falling in love with you, Anita. I'm glad I found you."

Anita whispered, "Me, too. Your friendship has been a wonderful blessing in my life. We'll take it one day at a time, Tom. Thank you for loving me. Such an honor. I can't begin to explain all I feel for you but know it is endearing and marvelous and exciting and comfortable and most of all, right. This must be happening God's way in God's time."

Both had happy tears welling up from within. The moment was sweet and the future seemed even better.

They left the restaurant hand in hand. They walked along silently, lost in their thoughts and hopes. God knew they were praying to Him from the depths of their hearts. He was ready to answer, ready to unfold this important next step in their lives.

That night as Anita was on her knees praying her evening share time with God, she felt an overwhelming love in her heart for Tom. She could see that even though he was imperfect as all are, his heart belonged to His heavenly Father. This new love God was giving her for him was way beyond what she could find on her own. She thanked God for answering her. Eventually she fell asleep, peaceful.

Tom had known for a long time that Anita was the person God had chosen for him. There were too many unusual coincidences. He perceived a true obvious blending of ideals and interests. It was fun being together. She really delighted in serving the Lord.

He was so afraid he might lose her, he asked God to cover all their experiences together to honor Him. He hoped she would come to love him with that pure unselfish unconditional love he yearned for. He loved her deeply beyond understanding. He wanted to protect, comfort and share his life with her. He just wanted her to be sure.

The next time they met, they knew the answer they hoped for in the eyes of each other. Who can explain that pure floating joyful feeling of the love between two souls accepting the destiny chosen, the unknown paths of experiences waiting to be shared. Best of all, God promised to never leave nor forsake them. It was good. They talked and talked; laughed and laughed.

As Tom placed a sparkling diamond on Anita's finger about a week later, the world was put on notice that this girl was to be his bride, his responsibility, his shared future. This lovely girl was his best friend and had his heart completely.

Anita brought the diamond up close to her eyes and through this precious symbol of Tom's love, watched the rainbow lights being reflected from the world around her. She then kissed Tom lovingly and just didn't want to stop it felt so right, so good. She thanked him for his deep devotion. The promise of life together under God was the answer to her dreams and the desire of her heart.

CHAPTER 5

The Wedding

Two months later everything came together. Anita and Tom had planned a quiet June wedding in the chapel of the Mattapan Methodist church.

Each person participating in the ceremony had a part in the total plan of God for this beautiful couple.

Anita's bridesmaids were her best friends Jennie and Ethel. They were like family to her. Her junior bridesmaid was her younger sister, Ruthie; her matron of honor, her older sister, Eunice. Tom's little niece, seven-year-old Susan, was the flower girl. All were dressed in soft dusty rose chiffon. Susan's twin brother, Russell was the ring bearer. The twins were pretty excited and took their responsibilities seriously. They'd do anything to watch their Uncle Tom smile in approval. Tom's best man was his older brother, Joe. His groomsmen were Pastor Golden, his minister; Frank, Jennie's husband and Larry, Ethel's husband.

Two families were coming together, surrounded by love.

Pastor Baker was glad to see such a joyous occasion. Being able to officiate at Tom and Anita's wedding was one of the highlights of his life. He had known Anita since she was a little girl and saw a life committed to God and family. He saw how Tom loved her beyond measure. Life might not be easy for them, but neither one seemed afraid of hard work. They were open to God's leadings.

He thought it all over in his study, "This is what is supposed to be. This is evidence of lives committed to the Lord and now to each other. I wish more couples were as well prepared for marriage. This should last."

The two mothers, both widows, were watching the fulfillment of their dreams for their beloved children. They noticed their other children and their families were seated. The two beloved fathers were not physically present but maybe God was letting them watch from heaven. There were many guests, trying to settle in just waiting to see the entrance of the bride.

There was soft organ music adding to the beauty of the gathering. The afternoon sunbeams were being filtered through stained glass windows depicting the life of Jesus.

As the mothers were escorted to their seats, the string quartet played

Tom entered from the side door with his brother, Joe, and Pastor Baker.

The procession was like a moving melody. Sweet faces coming down the aisle, two by two. The flower girl gently scattered white and pink rose petals.

At last, Anita appeared on her Uncle Fred's arm. When Tom saw her, he felt his heart racing a bit. Everything and everybody turned into a blur except for the girl he loved so deeply slowly walking toward him. She was entering a new life with him and they would find completeness in each other.

The moment they touched hands, he wanted to kiss her right away, but this was a sacred moment. First they were to pray and make promises to God and each other. Anita looked into Tom's eyes and saw precious love and tears of joy only for her.

Pastor Baker went through the familiar parts of the ceremony. He spoke of the love for God in each of their hearts. He spoke of searching and finding God's plan for their lives. In the day to day succession of experiences, they were to face all problems with unconditional love, forgiveness, selflessness and, of course, joy. Their lives would make a difference in the world and could help bring many souls to the Father in heaven. They were to find their God-given pathway, making angels rejoice.

The promises were made; the rings exchanged; prayers and music and then when Pastor Baker declared them married, everyone clapped. They had witnessed an unforgettable moment for Tom and Anita.

The endearing couple had an unusual beginning getting to know each other in the first place. They loved figuring out how God pushed them along on their shared adventure called life. Never would they take each other for granted. Seeking God's wisdom daily would be one of the keys to facing the future.

During the buffet dinner, Tom asked Anita to just sit down and relax a bit. They had been dancing and visiting with all the guests.

They had been laughing with their friends and needed to just stop and eat something. Joe made a dedication to the couple as did several others. After the cake cutting, Anita put a small piece of paper in Tom's hand. Tom read it and put it away in his wallet. It was their new phone number and her new name. He put it right next to two other little notes that had changed his life.

"Now I have the best little note in the world from the best little wife a man could ever want." He could not resist holding her gently and kissing her with passion. Anita almost lost her breath with all his endearments, but why stop? She just felt so good, so right, so loved.

Before long, the music ended, people had to leave, the many gifts were carefully brought to their new apartment nearby. Many family tears and hugs ended the day. Tom and Anita went to their new home, changed into traveling clothes and began their honeymoon adventure.

How can we possibly go through their lives together?

It was an adventure.

CHAPTER 6

Friends Forever

Jennie and Ethel had their adventures also. God kept them from soul crippling events. In time each found the husband God had chosen. They found the perfect plan for their lives.

Jennie followed her dream of learning to sing better. She joined the choir while still a teenager. She loved being in chorus in high school and later at Boston University. She majored in Communications and minored in Music. Every Sunday was dedicated to church activities and she made many friends. She sang solos often and faithful Anita was her accompanist.

She had a knack for organization and helped plan youth get-togethers at the park, the beach and even up some mountain trails nearby. Such a beautiful talented young lady emanated vitality. She wanted her life to count for good. Her love for God and simple kind ways made her irresistible to one of the young bachelors.

Frank had decided to be pretty choosy about getting to really know any of the girls. Many were silly or self-centered. In contrast, Jennie seemed genuine and helpful. He caught her secret special smile just for him whenever they met at church. Talking with each other was comfortable. She liked music and he was getting to be pretty good "fiddling", a common name for playing the violin. He respected her high ideals that easily matched his own. They went for casual walks together along the shady streets of Mattapan. Once he invited her to see a play in Boston, another time they went to a concert.

Frank's uncle was a successful businessman, venturing into new activities that held promise for the future. Often he would include Frank in management duties. The young man was just out of college, bright, showed good judgment, was trustworthy and had good accounting skills. He was like the son he never had. The future seemed to be unfolding.

Silent movies attracted the attention of the common people. It was like a theater experience, only costing less. Frank and his uncle saw enormous opportunities bringing excitement and happiness to others. In a short time, they found themselves with two "movie theaters" to manage. Frank was in charge of one of them. To make his theater outstanding, he brought in a piano. He found piano players who could keep up with the movie and bring emotion to the stories presented. Sometimes, he would take out his "fiddle" and play along.

There were a few times, he couldn't find a piano player and Jennie's dear friend, Anita, was glad to help out. She always did a great job but her time was limited. Since her father died, she had many new responsibilities at home.

Frank and Jennie soon realized they were in love. As time wore on, they saw how God had been preparing them for each other. They were glad they waited for the right person. No one is perfect, they knew, but unconditional love covers any problem.

Their wedding was held at the Arboretum under tall oak trees. The beauty of nature surrounded the wedding party and guests. There were flowering bushes everywhere. It was the beginning of a long joyful musical marriage. Their future children were to be great blessings in the family and church happenings. There were four and each sang well and played musical instruments.

Ethel had plenty of excitement in her life. She was just drawn toward Larry, one of the teens that were part of the mission to Appalachia. When he spoke back in 1911 at the youth rally, she listened. Her heart listened also to an endearing person truly dedicated to God. Everything he said seemed so right.

Two years later, she signed up to go on the next missions project in the same general area. She knew there would be plenty of exhausting physical work and ministry. She was a little worried it might be too difficult but since Anita agreed to go with her, she took courage saying, "My new adventure!" That seemed to settle it. She was glad Larry would be there. She knew this is what he did every summer.

There was plenty of hard work. Ethel thrived on challenges. Her adventurous spirit was infectious and she helped many go way beyond what they thought they could do. She brought a lot of love to the mountain folk. She appreciated their skills and knowledge of uses of the herbs and plants there. They taught her a bit about their special crafts and Ethel shared some great sewing projects .Their openness to the messages of the Bible brought a spirit of holiness to the evening meetings.

Larry could not help but notice this vivacious girl, always laughing, never afraid of working hard, always bringing cheer. He and Ethel were able to get well acquainted as they helped to build a safe meeting house in a long forgotten neighborhood in the back hills. The mountain families back there had unsafe homes. Some were ready to collapse in the winter when the snow fell for hours and hours, weighing down the rooftops. The new meeting house was to be a place of refuge. Always there would be warmth and food. Also it was to be a place for the women to help each other to pursue their crafts, make quilts, sew clothes and make fruit preserves from all the abundant berries in the hills. Church services and Bible studies groups could gather there.

Ethel loved talking with the women and children who had welcomed them. They were shy but she noticed they genuinely appreciated the project visit.

She and Anita tried to get everyone, men and women alike, singing some of the old hymns. There were many who could not read, but they remembered music from their past. One of the men had even added a few verses to some old favorites. It was good.

Each of the last three years, Larry had assumed a leadership role, matching the talents of each worker with the jobs to be done. This year on many occasions, he made sure he matched his own talents with Ethel's. Maybe he did it subconsciously, but who knows what could happen when a young man falls in love. Anita could see Ethel responding to the many little Larry attentions.

Before long it became obvious that Larry and Ethel were a match made in heaven. Oh, how they loved the Lord; oh, how they loved serving others. They brought out the best in each other. Their ideas together were better than their ideas separately.

Eventually, they were married and had four children. They thanked God for bringing them together. Larry studied and become a minister. He encouraged many of the youth at his churches to serve the less fortunate.

CHAPTER 7

After 50 Years

It was Boston in February 1961.

The chill in the air was not too bad, but sensible folks made sure to wear hats, scarves, gloves and warm coats.

Not too many people noticed an older graying couple walking along together in the Boston Commons. They were carefully bundled up and held hands lovingly. Every now and then they would stop and sit awhile. They seemed happy together smiling at others, sharing a nice greeting or a word of encouragement. They even went up to some lonely people and put a little booklet and some chocolate candies in their hands.

"Let's go to our own donut place. I wonder if it is still there."

Yes, it was Tom himself now in his sixties still in love with his beautiful wife at his side. His gray hair was full and framed a kind face. Not too many wrinkles, but the few that showed emphasized his smile and happy eyes. Many wondered why he never had the usual worry lines like so many of his age.

Anita was enjoying this walk down memory lane with Tom. Her large hazel eyes still sparkled. Her hair was almost all white, her skin still soft. She had a few wrinkles, but Tom called them laughy lines and kissed them often.

They walked a little further down the street and Anita exclaimed, "Tom, look over there. It looks a little different but I just know that is our old donut shop."

"Great! Let's go."

It was good to get into a nice warm place, smelling of coffee and cinnamon.

Before long they were settled into a nice corner booth drinking coffee.

"Look at all the kinds of donuts, Tom. I think I'll always love the glazed donuts the most. Look at the wall. They still have the same saying we remember, "Wherever you may wander, whatever be your goal, keep your eyes upon the donut and not upon the hole."

Tom got up went to the counter and bought a pair of glazed donuts. They were still warm and Anita said," Oh, that tastes really good."

Tom started thinking about their lives together. "You know, dear, that bit of philosophy got us through some tough times. It is the same as focusing on the positive ways of God, not on the tricks of the devil. God is like the donut, evil like the hole. God's part gives strength, evil is just empty."

Anita loved how Tom could find a holy lesson in everything that happened. God found the two were usually open to Him and teachable.

That brought humility and a peaceful attitude to each circumstance of life.

It was time to return home. The children would be waiting.

The children, oh, their precious children with children of their own.

Every time they could get together was exhausting but in a good way. It was their son, Donald's 39th birthday. His loving wife, Marion, wanted to celebrate with a nice dinner and cake for the whole family. Their children had made special gifts for their Dad. Tom and Anita had a daughter, Ruthanne, who would be coming over with her husband and their three boys.

Tom and Anita had just returned that Christmas from a seven year missions project in Peru. It was time to take it a bit easy and not miss out any more on being with their grandchildren. Life was getting harder for everyone as the years went by. Don and Marion's home was very big and they redesigned one part of the upstairs into a comfortable apartment for their aging parents. The couple could be independent but close enough to family to be watched and helped as needed.

Now the party was about to begin.

By the time Tom and Anita were returning home, it had became so cold, it almost hurt. When they arrived, there was a nice fire going in the fireplace. The whole family welcomed them in. The children flocked around their grandparents, jumping up and down, squealing with delight.

Who could resist such love? Coats and gloves were put away in the apartment upstairs. Then Grandma and Grandpa descended down to the main living room. Tom brought along his precious violin and set it down on a special stand over by the piano.

Pretty soon the dinner was ready and what a joy to see all eleven family members around the table. Donald spoke the blessing, so thankful for another year of life, the food God provided and the opportunity to be together. The children chattered on and on about their lives. Tom and Anita were surprised the meal was chicken casserole and salad.

"Do you remember one unusual time we had this?" Tom asked. He started to laugh and no one knew why, except Anita.

"How can I ever forget? Remember the red and white checkered tablecloths and the daisies in the blue glass vases? I can never forget that day." Anita smiled and chuckled. She remembered how God in His infinite wisdom made a good thing out of a wrong action. She knew that was mercy.

"What are you talking about?" asked the children.

"Oh, never mind, honey bunches, just something between Grandpa and me."

When it came time for the cake and candles, everyone sang Happy Birthday to Donald. Then Tom and Anita sang the Mañanitas song in Spanish they learned while in Peru.

Marion laughed remembering something like that in Spanish classes in high school years before.

She announced, "If we have cake, we have ice cream, too."

The children yelled, "Yeah for ice cream, yeah for cake, yeah for birthdays." Dutifully, Donald blew out all the candles, first try. He was good. His eyes twinkled a bit like his Dad's when he saw chocolate chip ice cream coming to the table.

After supper and the presents were opened, Tom suggested a little family sing- along. He picked up his violin and Anita sat down at the piano.

It was a rare treat to hear music from this talented duo. They would take a deep breath and one would start, the other following right on, right pitch and right on time. As their hearts seemed to beat as one, their music blended seamlessly. For years they had brought the word of God to others through hymns and songs, as well as by speaking the truth in love.

They started with, "He's got the whole world in His hands." The children loved that and sang along clapping their hands. Soon each child had a favorite and it blessed the older couple that the requests were good Sunday School songs and had been important in their own lives also, such as "Jesus Loves Me", "We're Marching to Zion", "A Wonderful Savior is Jesus My Lord", "Trust and Obey", "I Come to the Garden Alone"., "I've got the joy, joy, joy, joy down in my heart" "I'd Rather have Jesus than Silver or Gold." Different family members shared what the songs meant to them and how it helped them when facing decisions. Ruthanne remarked how the song, "What a Friend We Have in Jesus" gave her inner strength during a lonely time when she was away at college. Her husband mentioned "All to Jesus I surrender" as his personal song when he dedicated his whole heart to Jesus.

It was important to share what God had revealed to each family member. Tom and Anita could see answers to their daily prayers covering their children and grandchildren. It was good to remember and repeat many Bible verses.

Singing helped a lot also. Sometimes people would learn and sing melodies, and later on, singing it again, the meaning of the verses would come alive in their souls. In the Bible, there was a part where Jesus, himself, sang. Most likely it was a praise song to God, His Father.

The evening ended. Ruthanne and her family bundled up, shared hugs and left for their home in the next town. Don and Marion sat by the fireplace not wanting the evening to end. The children went off to bed.

Tom and Anita were tired and helped each other up the stairs to their own special place. They got ready for bed. Even though their bodies seemed worn out, their minds were racing. Memories flooded their thoughts.

Life had been an adventure. Their friendship turned into a deep abiding love. A beautiful wedding began years and years of serving the Lord together. Tom's violin playing and Anita's gift for playing the piano turned out to be a blessing for many.

Through the years, they enjoyed keeping in touch with many dear friends. Experiences and adventures enriched their lives. By honoring God, they found peace and God's perfect plan.

As Tom had continued teaching in the elementary school, he did extra studies, earning a Master's degree in Educational Leadership.

No one was surprised when he was awarded the position of principal of that same school. He had a sincere desire to challenge the children there to strive for excellence. "Work hard with integrity, help and respect others" were the mottos he fought for in all his education meetings.

Anita was glad she could be a stay- at- home wife. She made a beautiful home life for Tom. Eventually, their children, Don and Ruthanne, came into their lives. It was a constant challenge to fight off evil influences in the world. Giving their hearts to Jesus was definitely the highlight of their children's existence. The little family of four found ways of reaching out to the poor and unfortunate. They chose the path of sharing and giving of their time.

Years rolled by and Don and Ruthanne found spouses that God had chosen. This all came about as a result of prayer, soul searching and patience. They in turn had children of their own, the same ones they had just hugged at the birthday celebration.

Tom and Anita watched their children leave and make their own homes. Instead of slowing down for an easier life God put in their hearts to go on with something new. They had the gifts of music, time, energy, patience and most of all, love

It was time to let go of worldly possessions to follow the path of righteousness.

Tom and Anita sold or gave away most of their lifelong accumulation of things. They knew that people were more important than things, anyway. They were accepted to be part of a Methodist missions team to go to Peru. They had been studying Spanish together for a couple of years. They were offered a job in a bilingual school there, Tom to teach history and geography, Anita to help in the music ministry. They promised to go and had support for three years.

They went. What they did was so appreciated, those three years stretched into seven. Who can explain the joys and trials living in another country? It took a while to accept and embrace the differences and learn how best to serve others. That unconditional love really helped. Constant study in the Bible gave meaning to life. The best part was Tom and Anita had each other still. It was still pretty exciting knowing God had all of this planned out. So much was never imagined during the early years.

It was good, now, to be back with the family in their beloved country.

Tom covered Anita's hand with his.

It was time to give thanks to God.

It was time to go to sleep

It was time to rest in the Lord.

"He brought us through His plan for our lives."

Anita added, "We're ready for whatever is next. Good night, sweetheart."

"God bless you, 'night."

A few miles away, there was another couple, Jennie and Frank, also thanking God for their own lives together. They had been a major support for Tom and Anita in Peru the whole seven years. Their theaters no longer showed silent movies. No more need for violin and piano playing to enhance the action. Frank kept his theaters family friendly and refused to show horror or violent productions. He made his choices to honor God.

Jenny directed the choir and sang often at their church. Their children were following in their footsteps. It was all in the plan of God. They were blessed.

Jenny and Frank were forever thankful to have found each other, so as to honor God together.

Ethel and Larry now lived in a retirement home in Central Florida. Arthritis and just old age had slowed them down. They had established a foundation to support the creative skills of the mountain people. Also there were five annual scholarships given to hard working promising teens from the part of Appalachia where the Methodist missions teams served. They cherished the memories of the years of establishing the foundation, of getting to know and love the mountain people. All of this was in the plan of God.

The plan of God is different for each person. However, the result is the same. We are to serve God and others with love. God will turn mistakes around for His glory. People need humble teachable hearts that repent when there are wrong choices and resulting sad consequences. All have sinned, no one is perfect. Compassion, forgiveness and unconditional love should be the way of life. One day all Christians will want to hear from their Lord, "Well done, thou good and faithful servant." We then enter into a whole new life. We enter into heaven.

Love for stories

As a young lady, my mother, Bessie Hackley, loved to write stories and many were published in the newspapers during the 1920'S. Then, after she married and had her two children, Donald and me, I can remember joyful times every evening when she and Dad would read books and tell stories to us (back in the 1930's and 1940's). So it is no surprise that I always loved writing stories at school and being the neighborhood storyteller. As the years are passing, I am still loving writing stories. Many times they seemed to write themselves. My inner soul and love for God and for others always seem to reaching out to be a blessing.

One of my children, Benjamin SanMartin, has a gift for writing and I want to share a piece he showed me.

Remembering a trail

Not much to do today, I thought, emerging from the tent. It was crisp and clear, the air thin and blowing lightly from the Northwest. Looking around I see the weathered rocks with vegetation growing from the cracks.

The ground seemed busy with squirrel. Walking now down the path, no sound, only the pitch of the wind racing through the trees. It was Fall as I approached the Aspen. Just the sound of my boots walking down the path as I entered this forest of thin white pillars known as the Aspen. It sounds different now, the wind through the trees humming from all directions. Glancing slightly upward and noticing some leaves blowing across my path from left to right. Ears a little cold, feeling the bite of the cold air with every breath. Stopping now, slowly looking around, just me, gazing upward now and noticing the sky above. A crisp and deep blue sky, no clouds, just a pure and perfect blue with the golden leaves of the Aspen stretching upwards and swaying slightly in the wind. "My God", I say quietly to myself, "have you ever seen anything so beautiful?" Embracing the moment and wondering how people could ever believe that all this creation was just a random act of science.

Moving on now, I see an opening ahead; it looks like an overlook. Getting closer, I begin to realize the majestic view that I'm approaching. Taking a few careful steps over the rocks with sound of the trees behind me now, I look up slowly to see a panoramic view of towering mountains with snow on their peaks. The valley below where the gold of the Aspen meanders through the Blue Spruce and Evergreen like a rich gold vein on a rock face. A clearing below where a small herd of elk is resting and grazing in peace. The world before me has exploded with color and natural wildlife.

These are the Rocky Mountains of Colorado, a place I dream of so frequently. A place I've been, enjoyed, experienced in many ways. It all seems like a dream now, so distant and far away.

The memories remain fresh, the scent of the air, the sounds, the majesty.

One day I will return and experience it again.

Not much to do today, so I remember.

*

I loved this short piece he wrote.

A message to my readers

I hope you like this my first volume of stories for children and families. Some are based in part on real experiences, others with what could have been. Long after you read these stories, their word pictures will return and you will find courage as you face life.

You can write me if you wish at

Westbow Press

1663 Liberty Drive

Bloomington, IN 47403

USA

Author's Biography

Shirley Duke SanMartin grew up in Randolph, Massachusetts; graduated from Thayer Academy and Massachusetts School of Art; and then married her beloved husband, Dr. Raul SanMartin. Five children, five grandchildren and five great grandchildren later, she enjoys following her heart. She loves God, family, and everyone she meets. She continues her creativity in writing and painting.

*

Sending love to all my readers
Shirley Duke SanMartin
2018
Only one life
'Twill soon be past
Only what's done for Christ
Will last

Printed in the United States
by Bookmasters

Printed in the United States
By Bookmasters